Georgia + Harrison,

foll

10

Shadow Cote

30/6/19

BRILLIANT
CHALLENGES

JOHN THOMAS CROWLEY

Typeset by handebooks.co.uk

Order of Characters

Naeku
Charlie
Anaru
Saif and Zahid
Guia

Also by John Thomas Crowley

Great Rescues
Meeting V.I.Ps
The Smarter Kids

NAEKU

The black, saturated storm clouds that had gathered over the plains of the Maasai Mara National Park for the last few hours were about to burst. A dazzling electrical storm would ensue, lighting up the African skies like a firework display. The deluge of rain that would come tumbling out of the sky would quickly turn the dried-out plains to a muddy quagmire. Riverbeds that had been dry for months would become raging torrents of cascading waters. With the fresh rains invigorating the plains, the parched lands would be transformed into a vast green carpet of vegetation. The scent of the new grasses that were carried on the wind would be picked up by the migrating herds of wildebeest, zebra and antelope already making their way north through the great Serengeti plains. This migration of hundreds of thousands of animals that followed the scents of fresh grasses was one of the world's greatest spectacles, as witnessed by overhead satellite images that were beamed into our homes via the TV, smartphones, YouTube and many other social media outlets.

The sight of the migrating herds entering their territories was good news to the resident predators, signalling the hard times of famine were over and a period of feasting was about to begin as a glut of food came their way. Lions, cheetahs, hyenas and wild dogs often timed the birth of their cubs or pups to coincide with this time of plenty, thus giving their young a fighting chance in life, but the poachers with their cunning and devious ways would be there too.

Naeku sat on the veranda that ran across the back of her house; she was grumbling to herself as the house wi-fi was playing up. The websites she was looking at were either taking forever to download or simply freezing with the buffering symbol going round and round in the middle of the screen. She was getting annoyed and starting to lose patience with her laptop. Tomorrow was going to be an important day for her; she was going to meet her grandfather for the first time and she wanted to show him that she had some knowledge of her heritage. Her grandfather was the chief village elder of a small Maasai community, living a simple life in a small kraal close to one of the seven main crossing points that the African migrating herds used to cross the mighty Mara River. She wanted to know more about the Maasai people and their customs so she could impress the man she had seen in the only photo she had of him, dressed in full Maasai warrior robes. Her father talked very little about his father; they had fallen out sometime ago about his decision to give up the pastoral, semi-nomadic ways of the traditional Maasai people, opting for a career in medicine and a more comfortable modern way of life. The wealthy suburbs of Nairobi, the capital of Kenya where she had been brought up, would be a far cry from a dusty kraal of mud huts close to the Kenyan-Tanzanian border in the Maasai Mara reserve. But she couldn't wait to go; her father was understandably a little anxious as he was going to see his father for the first time in twenty years.

The 4x4 Jeep, driven by her father, pulled off the dirt track that led to the kraal; Naeku stepped out, wearing her latest designer clothes and trainers. Her father had warned her not to expect luxury accommodation with the latest internet connections. The traditional bomba (house) that her grandfather lived in was a simple affair of timber poles fixed directly into the ground and interwoven with a lattice of branches that were covered with a mix of cow dung, mud and human urine. It was late morning when Naeku and her father finally got to meet her grandfather, as he had been out talking with other village elders about the spate of cattle rustling and recent lion and cheetah attacks on his livestock. She was slightly nervous as he approached. He was a tall elegant man dressed in the traditional Maasai red shuka with cowhide sandals on his feet. In Maasai terms he was wealthy, as he had over a hundred cattle and numerous children, but compared to her own father he was an uneducated poor man; nevertheless she had chosen to spend the next few weeks getting to know this man and his ways.

Her father and grandfather exchanged polite conversation, but it was clear for all to see that a tension existed between them and her father chose to leave by early evening. With her father gone, Naeku set about getting to know her new family.

The following morning her grandfather sat her down under a tree, the very spot where he had sat with other children he had grown up with listening to his teacher. School in his day was a few rickety desks and chairs set out under a big ash tree, providing some shade from the overhead sun; his education was limited. Nowadays the school bus picks the village children up from the end of the dirt track, taking them to the nearby government centre. From there the children progressed to the universities in Nairobi. Her grandfather suggested that she changed out of her expensive clothes and put on suitable Maasai attire, as they would be walking together all day out on the plains to see the wildlife.

Sitting to her right, propped against the bough of the big ash tree, he asked:

"Why have you come?"

"To find out more of my culture, and to see for myself the destruction mankind is bringing on the natural habitat and the wildlife. Is the plight of some of our endangered species as bad as portrayed by the TV images shown on our screens, grandfather?"

Olekina and his sister Lankenua were twins; they lived in the last bomba in the kraal near the enkang (outer fence). Olekina was intrigued as to why his grandfather was taking so much interest in this outsider. For a ten year old his curiosity often got the better of him, invariably getting him into trouble with his patriarchs. He and his grandfather often had to have words over his annoying antics and general boyish behaviour.

"I think the best way for us to talk about what

you want to know is to take a walk out onto the plains."

"Will we be safe, grandfather?"

"As long as you follow my instructions, we'll be safe. It's dangerous out there; you need to respect nature's ways. Watch and listen for the warning signs, but most importantly stick by my side."

Olekina, who had conveniently placed himself within eavesdropping distance, pretending to be busy doing nothing, scurried off to find his sister.

"Olekina!"

"Yes, Gramps."

"Grandfather to you, cheeky monkey. I suppose you've overheard that I am taking Naeku out into the bush."

"No, Grandfather."

"Hmm… One of these days, young man, your tongue and sharp wit will get you into serious trouble. Pack a rucksack, fetch your sister and be at the enkang gate in twenty minutes."

"I didn't see Olekina sneak up on us."

"You wouldn't; he's good at that. We don't call him the village gossip for nothing. If you want to spread a rumour, tell Olekina; it will be round the village and the surrounding hills within minutes. Sometimes he has his uses."

"How?"

"Oh… you know. If I want to know what's going on around here and the outlying villages there's no point asking the other elders of the village; they won't know. I ask Olekina and, if he doesn't know, he'll sure find out and get back to me. You see, Naeku, I don't need that internet and smartphone stuff; I have Olekina."

The overhead sun was powerful; most of the big cats and other predators would be sitting or sleeping under any shade they could find. Exerting energy chasing prey in full view and in the heat of the day was futile and stupid. The wildebeest, zebra and gazelles had the upper hand with their agility and speed and thousands of lookouts. By night the cats had the advantage as they generally had better night vision than the herd animals, plus it was cooler and the darkness provided the necessary cover to get up close to their target before pouncing and attacking.

Sticking to the well-trodden tracks used by the Maasai for centuries, just like their big cat neighbours do, the three children walked single file behind their grandfather. As they walked the old man began to tell them some of the stories that had been passed down from one generation to the next: how their forefathers from the Nilotic peoples had originated from the lower Nile valley, north of Lake Turkana around South Sudan and Ethiopia, how they had a fearsome reputation as warriors and cattle rustlers. He went on talking about the Maasai traditions and how those traditions were fading fast as many of the younger generation had left the family homesteads and headed for the big cities of Nairobi and Dar Es Salaam for a different life. For him, he would adhere to the Maasai ways until he died and was left out for the vultures to have their say.

Naeku spotted two young male lions perched on a small outcrop of rock no more than fifty metres away to her right; they looked nervous as they surveyed the migrating herds spread out beneath them from their vantage point. Lankenua watched them for a few minutes; they were probably two brothers who, for the first time in their young lives, had to defend and provide for themselves as a result of being kicked out of a local pride. They would have every right to be nervous, as they would be attacked and killed by the dominant male of this territory they had invaded if found; a scenario they would have to get used to until they were bigger and strong enough to fight for their own pride and patch of land.

"Grandfather."

"Yes, Lankenua, I think they are the lions that have been attacking our cattle."

The old man recalled that the villages had reported sightings of two young males new to the area that had been attacking their stock. Olekina would find out and report back.

It was nearing forty degrees and the midday sun sat high in the sky above the plains. The old man headed for the outcrop of rock that the two young male lions had temporarily claimed; he knew how to scare them off, but the view across the Mara plains would be spectacular and the shade of the four trees there would be welcome. Sitting under the shade of the trees and watching the thousands of wildebeest and zebra crisscrossing the vast plains that stretched out as far as the eye could see below them was truly amazing, Mother Nature at her best. Naeku simply sat and took in everything around her; her grandfather continued with his stories and his thoughts for the Maasai generations that would follow in his footsteps.

A small cheetah family, a young mother and her three cubs, sat aloft on a small heap of earth, most likely the remnants of an old abandoned termite mound. The old grandfather could tell she was eyeing up a small zebra calf or gazelle and was getting ready for her next kill; she had three small cubs to feed so there was no midday snooze for her, not like the lazy lion prides that camped in her territory. They would be sprawled out flat on their backs, legs in the air, still digesting last night's meal with not a care in the world.

The three children sat transfixed as the thrill of the hunt was on; the mother cheetah slipped off the mound, snarling at her cubs to do the same and hide themselves in the long grass until she returned. The mother cheetah had positioned herself downwind of her victim, a zebra calf, slowly stalking forward inch by inch, blade by blade of grass. Crouching down, eyes locked on the calf, she sprang. The calf, crying for its mother's protection, ran for its life. Naeku had her hands over her mouth, screaming to herself, desperately hoping that the little calf would outpace the mother cheetah with its zigzagging, twisting, turning, ducking and diving. It was all over within minutes. A cloud of dust that was thrown up into the air was the signal the chase was over; the little cheetah cubs would be having lunch shortly. The old grandfather turned to his grandchildren:

"One animal's loss is another animal's gain; that's Mother Nature's rules here on the great African plains."

Naeku looked at her grandfather with teary eyes; she knew the ways of life here in the bush, but it was still hard to see a little life snuffed out so violently.

Nightfall was close at hand; their grandfather, once a proud fighting warrior, knew it wasn't safe out on the plains at night because the big cats and other predators would be stirring themselves for the nightly business of hunting prey. The night's cast of characters would soon be emerging from their burrows to face whatever the night threw at them, and those animals that had endured the punishing heat and dust of the day would be looking for a safe place to rest. With a bit of luck they might see the morning again.

Walking back the track they had come, Naeku heard a commotion from behind a clump of bushes; a group of youths had gathered, sitting on quad bikes smoking whatever. Naeku and her cousins knew exactly what these yobs were up to. They were the unscrupulous poachers, who didn't care about the animals they harmed as long as the illegal traffickers paid them. They killed or stole to order; their ill-gotten gains they would spend buying flash bikes or the latest designer gear from the posh shops in Nairobi.

The old grandfather whispered to Olekina:

"Take your sister and Naeku back to the kraal. Get a message to the park rangers and tip them off as to my whereabouts and don't come back. Do you hear me?"

"Yes grandfather, whatever."

The old grandfather knew in his heart Olekina would be back and that he would probably be sweet talking Naeku and his sister to do likewise at this precise moment. He shrugged his shoulders in utter despair; he loved Olekina but knew one day he'd come a cropper. The old warrior nudged his way through the bushes so as to get a closer look at the yobs; he recognised some of them and would be talking to the elders of their villages. As far as he could ascertain there weren't many rifles. Only one of them was armed; he would be the lookout, so he assumed they were not on a mission to kill the rhinos or elephants for their horns and tusks tonight. The cloth bags that were scattered on the ground hinted they were after cubs, mainly cheetah cubs, as they fetched a good price on the black market. The cubs' destination? Rich Arabs in the Gulf states, where the cheetah was a highly prized fashion symbol, a must-have object prowling the immaculately manicured gardens of the wealthy or in the front seats of their BMWs and Mercs.

Olekina had done his job; the park rangers had arrived at the kraal within the hour, anxious to get going and catch the poachers red-handed. The head ranger turned to Naeku: "Send a text to your grandfather. Tell him we're on our way and to text back with his location."

Before Naeku could open her mouth, Olekina butted in: "You're having a laugh! 'Texting!' That old man wouldn't know how to switch a phone on! We'd better show you the way."

With a cheeky right-eyed wink at Naeku and his sister, it was mission accomplished! They were off for some action.

The blazing heat of the day had given way to a chilly night; the overhead moon gave some light to what could only be described as a pitch-black sky. Naeku was amazed at the thousands of stars that glittered high up in the night's stratosphere; yes, she could see the stars from her bedroom window back at home, but the city lights would dim the view; here on the great African plains of the Maasai Mara, away from the big city, the night sky was stunning. Naeku was walking behind the head ranger, keeping her torch directed at the ground as instructed; the decision had been taken not to take the park jeeps, as the lights and the noise of the engines would spook the poachers, giving them time to escape into the night on their bikes. The walk to the edge of the Mara River from the kraal was dangerous. The nightly sounds of the plains sent a shiver down Naeku's spine; she wished she was tucked up in her own bed Facebooking her friends. A nearby pride of lions roared into the night, letting everybody know of their presence; in the distance the low rumblings of a herd of elephants could be heard as they called out messages of reassurance to each other.

Naeku's grandfather was sitting in a tree as they

approached; scrambling down, he greeted the park rangers, informing them that the poachers had gone off into the bush. He had heard the young lads discussing their tactics; it was the three cheetah cubs they had spotted earlier that afternoon they had in mind as their next target.

One of the rangers asked how far ahead the poachers were. Naeku's old warrior grandfather speculated that the men were probably a few hundred metres ahead.

"How many are we talking about? Are they armed?" asked the head ranger.

"Four, and I recognise the stickers on the bikes; they come from a neighbouring village. I think one or two at the most are armed," replied Olekina.

Olekina's grandfather simply nodded.

"Naeku, Olekina, do you know where the mother cheetah and the cubs are?" asked one of the rangers.

"Yes, under the small outcrop we sat on earlier."

A single gunshot rang out across the night plain. The park rangers raced towards where the shot had come from; the six rangers fired in the air as they charged forward, surrounding the gang of four. Having been taken completely by surprise, the poachers dropped the tied sacks that had the three cubs in and headed towards the river, but quickly ran into a wall of angry hippos that were emerging from the river for their nightly feed on the nearby grassy plain. Trapped by a wall of hippos, notorious for being the most dangerous animal in Africa, the poaching gang dropped their weapons and surrendered. Three of the rangers fired flares to head off the startled hippos, sending them scurrying back to the river.

Standing on the outcrop of rock, the old grandfather explained to Naeku and the twins the gang would have waited for the mother cheetah to head off hunting before approaching the cubs. The cubs' instinct would be to lie perfectly still in the face of danger. The net that was thrown over them would have prevented them from escaping the gang's clutches. The mother must have heard their cries for help, abandoned her hunt and headed back to protect her cubs. The gang heard her coming and, once she was in range, shot her. That was the gunshot they heard.

The park rangers acted quickly, cuffing all four of the poachers; the commotion would have attracted the attention of numerous predators who would soon be on the scene to investigate the goings-on, placing everybody in danger. Olekina shouted at Naeku and his sister to run and pick up the sacks with the cubs in. The cubs were heavy, and their wriggling around made it really difficult to get a firm grip of the sacks.

Naeku struggled with her cheetah cub, but she was determined to walk back to the kraal. She was angry with the poachers; they didn't care about what they had done tonight, they were simply annoyed with themselves for getting caught, which meant they would not be paid for their ill-gotten deeds and furthermore would be looking at a custodial sentence of several years in a Nairobi jail.

As for the three cheetah cubs; well, if left out on the plains without their mother's protection they would be dead within days, either killed by the lions or hyenas or simply dying from starvation. The loss of their mother would be devastating to these eight-week-old cubs; normally in the wild they would stay with their mother for up to eighteen months, learning all the necessary skills in life to become successful wild cheetahs. The rangers, like on so many occasions these days, were left with no option but to take the cubs to a specialised rescue centre for cheetahs; there they would be looked after and lovingly cared for by the staff. A training programme would be put in place over the next few years with the ultimate aim of releasing them back into the wild when the time was right. At least they had escaped the clutches of being some rich or famous person's pet trophy.

The last few weeks Naeku had spent with her grandfather learning about the Maasai ways and what was happening on the open plains had been an eye-opening experience, but now back in her bedroom, Naeku was looking on the internet as to find out what to do about the desperate plight of Africa's declining wildlife. Her father had said to her there was no point in being angry about what had happened; she needed to come up with a plan, something that would prick the conscience of world leaders as well as the rich and famous who saw the cubs as must-have accessories. Equally she would have to understand the mindset of the poachers and what led them to do the things they do, challenge and work with them. Invariably poverty was the driving force behind the poachers' actions and she would need to look at a programme of how to support them to get a better education and way of life. These challenges would be taxing, but if she really wanted to stop the mass destruction of the African wildlife she would have to work hard over the next few years.

A simpler challenge, though, was to work on her father, to start building a fresh relation with his father before it was too late.

That she would start tomorrow.

CHARLIE

Charlie looked out from his small attic bedroom window; he could see all the children from the street where he lived playing in the snow. He longed to join them, but the doctors had told him that his latest operation to rid the tumour that was wrapped around the base of his spine would take months of recuperation. A small red-breasted robin crash-landed on the windowsill, scratching at the snow to get at the last remaining seeds Charlie had put out that morning. As fast as the robin had appeared from the mists of nowhere he vanished; but not without a cheeky stare at the small boy on the other side of the windowpane as if to say, *'Thanks for the food mate.'* Charlie thought to himself; wow, wouldn't it be great to fly.

A knock at the front door of the house distracted Charlie for a few seconds; he could hear the voices of his best friends Peter, Ben and Rebecca in the hallway. His crutches were propped against the small bedside locker. A small photograph sat on top of the locker was recent; his dad had taken it in the park. It was a photo of himself and his friends the day before he went into hospital. His friends had signed the back of the frame: *'To Charlie, all our love Peter, Ben and Rebecca.'*

The clattering of his friends coming up the stairs reverberated around the whole house; normally they would all sit and play computer games, but today was different. It had snowed for the first time and it was proper snow. Peter threw Charlie his crutches while Ben looked out of the attic window.

"Guys, let's go tobogganing. Look, everybody is out on the park having fun."

The prospect of playing in the snow had excited them all, but a nagging thought crossed Charlie's mind. The doctors had told his parents to keep him safe from any winter colds, as his immune system was low from the operation and the subsequent chemo treatment he had endured over the last few weeks. He was fed up with sitting at home day after day while his friends went to school; he desperately wanted to go out in the snow and have some enjoyment in his life for a change. He knew his mother and father would disapprove; their answer would be *'Another day, son.'* Looking up at the window the little red-breasted robin had returned and was hopping on and off the windowsill; each time he landed he tapped the window with his beak as if to say, '*Come on Charlie, come out to play.*'

At that precise moment Charlie had made up his mind. He was going to venture out with his friends today. He knew that the snow would only be around for a couple of days before it turned to slush, and that his friends would be extremely disappointed having missed the opportunity to have fun in the snow. They wouldn't go unless he was with them. But: how to get past Charlie's mother?

Rebecca had an idea.

"I know! I'll phone my mum and tell her that Charlie's mother wants to meet for coffee as she has had some new ideas for the nearly new clothes shop they're thinking of opening. That should distract both of them for a few hours; they won't even notice we've gone."

Great idea, thought Ben; plan A was up and running.

Peter and Ben helped Charlie down the stairs while Rebecca checked to see that her mum and Charlie's were fully engrossed in the sitting room, discussing the new shop plans over two flat white coffees. Thumbs up gave the all clear for Peter and Ben to support Charlie down the remaining steps. Charlie got a fit of the giggles; this was the most excitement he had had in days. Ben elbowed Charlie in the ribs, at the same time whispering in his right ear to shut up.

Rebecca opened the cupboard door that was under the stairs, pulling Charlie's coat and scarf off the peg; his gloves had been stuffed into his pockets. Peter got the wheelchair which the hospital had loaned the family; it was next to the French windows in the dining room. Within minutes Charlie was kitted out for a snow adventure.

Charlie's house backed on to the park. The little gate at the bottom of the garden leading to the park was a bit of a rickety affair, but there, sitting on the post, was the small red-breasted robin observing the entire goings-on. The snow covering the garden path was proving difficult for Charlie to manage in his chair. Ben remembered his dad had chopped up some bits of wood for the old kitchen

Aga; in amongst the pile there were two small planks ideal for wooden skis.

"Where are you going, Ben?" shouted Peter.

"Back in a minute," mumbled Ben as he dashed across the park to his house.

The planks of wood were propped against the garage wall. Searching around he soon found some old rope and, looking up at his dad's tools that neatly hung on the wall, he saw the hammer and next to it on a small shelf his dad's red biscuit tin full of odd screws and nails. With all the clobber neatly tucked under his arms, he raced back across the park to Charlie's.

"What are you doing, Ben?" asked Charlie.

"Watch."

Charlie got out of his chair and, within a matter of moments Ben had converted the wheelchair into a supercharged sledge with the planks of wood acting as the runners. Ben had carefully threaded the rope through the wheel spokes and around the pieces of wood before finally nailing the rope to the planks for added support.

Rebecca was impressed with Ben's masterpiece; she leant towards him and gave him a little kiss on the cheek to say well done. Ben's blush didn't go unnoticed. Charlie and Peter simply giggled as Ben tried to hide his face in his gloves.

Kitted and booted out, the gang of four headed for the park. Hours of fun followed as Peter, Ben and Rebecca took it in turn to push Charlie in his newly converted sledge up the park slopes, jumping on him as the chair freely glided down the slopes in chase of the other children's toboggans. Tumbling out of his chair with whoever was sitting on his lap as they precariously careered down the slopes was exhilarating and fun. With all the thrills and spills no one had noticed the time; even the little red robin that was flying high above them was preoccupied with all the activity that was taking place below him.

The shrill voices of Charlie and Rebecca's mothers shouting their names from the top of the hill brought the day's proceedings to an abrupt end. Charlie looked at his friends and said, "I'm in for it now. I will say it was my idea and take the blame, but thank you so much. I haven't had so much fun in a day for a long time. I miss you all when you are at school and I'm stuck at home."

The retribution was swift; once home Charlie was banished to his room. He tried explaining to his mother that it was his decision to go out and not his friends', but she was not in the mood to listen to his story. She was angry with him and he knew why. Getting a cold, for him, was a serious matter.

Charlie looked out of his small attic window; the last of the daylight was disappearing and the man in the moon was already up in the sky. Waving goodnight to the little robin, still sitting on the gatepost as if he was keeping watch, he pulled his Doctor Who curtains to shut out the rest of the world. He had enjoyed a great day with his friends. This day would stay long in his memory, be it short or long; how long? Well, that would depend on how well the cancer responded to the treatment... For a nine-year-old boy he had a positive outlook on life. He knew he was seriously ill, and that his time on this planet might be shorter than his friends. But today was a great day and had put him in a better mood; ready to face the challenges ahead.

ANARU

Anaru was born in Dunedin, a city known for its Scottish and Maori heritage, on the east coast of South Island, New Zealand. His father's side of the family originated from Aberdeen in Scotland, arriving in New Zealand close to forty years ago. His mother's descendants could be traced back to one of the local Maori tribes around Rotorua on North Island. When he was born, his father had insisted in keeping the Scottish family traditional name of Andrew, but his mother wanted a Maori connection; hence the compromise. Anaru, the Maori for Andrew.

Queenstown, where Anaru grew up, was a small resort town that sat on the shore of Lake Wakatipu in Otago, a region in the south-west corner of South Island, New Zealand. The town itself was renowned for its sporting excellence; in winter the Southern Alps, the backbone of South Island that surrounded Queenstown, attracted thousands of skiers from around the world. In summer, G-force paragliding, trekking, hang gliding, water paragliding, jet skiing, parasailing and numerous other water sports attracted people in their thousands to the town and the lake. But for Anaru rugby was his sport; he passionately followed the Otago Highlanders, the area super rugby team based in Dunedin, going with his father to all the home games. The All Blacks Rugby Union team were not only the most dominant force in the southern hemisphere, but they held the number one slot in the world rankings. Anybody that followed rugby, be that Union or League, knew about The All Blacks. He would sit with his father and friends in the bars of Queenstown in his All Black T-shirt, glued to the TV screens watching the international games. His idol was Dan Carter, fly-half, the position he loved to play.

His mother was getting concerned about him and, having spoken with his father, an appointment was made for Anaru to attend the local doctor's surgery. She explained the changes in Anaru's general behaviour, how he was exhausted coming home from school, the bruises on his body, lack of appetite, the numerous coughs and sore throats, the recent bout of pneumonia, that he was complaining his knee joints hurt. Her instincts were telling her that something more sinister was lurking in the background. She was right.

It had been nearly three years since he was diagnosed with leukaemia; he recalled the day that he sat in the consultant's room with the doctor confirming to his parents that all the tests they had run concluded he had leukaemia, specifically (A.L.L) Acute Lymphoblastic Leukaemia. A blood cancer. He distinctly remembered looking at his parents and watching the blood drain from their faces; he could even call to mind his father, who was sitting on his left, slumping in his seat and burying his head in his hands, his mother simply staring out of the window with a vacant look as if she had seen a ghost. He was nine years old at the time, a little boy who didn't fully understand what was happening to him or what was coming his way. Dr Smith, the consultant from Southlands Hospital in Invercargill, had suggested they make another appointment to discuss the options available, but more importantly to take time out for all of them to absorb the devastating news.

Dr Smith had said right from the start the treatment was going to be long and difficult. There would be good days and dark days, numerous trips back and forward from Queenstown to Southlands Hospital in Invercargill. The treatment would be varied, possibly ranging from chemotherapy and radiotherapy to a variety of drugs. All would depend on how Anaru reacted to the different treatments as to what the next course of action would be. The good news was that the leukaemia had been caught in its early stages and that the prognosis outcome was very good, eighty to ninety percent. However Anaru would be under Dr Smith's team for the next two to three years.

Sitting opposite his mother at the breakfast table in the large farmhouse kitchen, Anaru reached for the envelope his mother had slipped across the table. They both knew what the letter was about. The stamp had Invercargill branded all over it. It was from the hospital. It was hard to believe that three years had passed since that fateful day, but it had.

The letter was brief; Dr Smith had personally signed it. It was the letter he and his parents had been longing for; he had been given the all-clear, and Dr Smith didn't want to see him any more and that he would look out for his name on the team sheets of the Otago Highlanders matches and hopefully as an All Black, straddling the world stage representing New Zealand like his hero Dan Carter.

The farmhands were busy, as the sheep farm that had been in the family for decades was preparing for the summer shearing. Anaru's mother had organised the hired contractors that were due in the next few days to shear the six thousand Merino sheep. It would take the contractors the best part of two weeks working from dawn to dusk to accomplish the enormous task.

Anaru raced down the track down to Walter Peak, the sheep station on the lakeshore that was set up for the summer tourists to experience life on a sheep farm, plus get a posh meal in the fancy restaurant there at rip-off prices. If rich Americans and Europeans wanted to pay those prices, well, let them pay, thought Anaru. As he neared Walter Peak he could see the TSS Earnslaw, the old coal-fired steamship that criss crossed Lake Wakapitu several times a day bringing the tourists back and forth between here and Queenstown. The old steamship was some way out on the lake; on board were the sheep contractors that would spend the next few weeks on their farm. No shearing for Anaru this year; he had other plans now that he had been given the all-clear.

Anaru had texted his mates his wonderful news; he had taken a selfie of himself and his mother at the breakfast table holding up that letter and posted it on Facebook and Instagram. As he reached the small wooden jetty on the tiny shingle beach at Walter Peak his mobile phone kept pinging as the messages of '*Congratulations*' appeared on his screen.

Looking through his contact list on his phone, he came to Mr O'Connell; gently touching the screen over the number, the call was placed.

"Hello, who is it?"

"Mr O'Connell, it's Anaru."

"Hello son, what can I do for you?"

"I got the all clear from Dr Smith today. I know yesterday was the 16th of January and that was the last day of registering for the U14 team for 2016, but could you please make an exception? I have the fifty-five dollars subs and a letter of consent from my mother and father. I'm on my way now. Please Mr O'Connell; I won't let you down."

"Anaru, that is fantastic news. Meet me after lunch at the school gates."

"Thanks, Mr O'Connell."

As he put his phone down a message flashed across its screen.

"Welcome to Wakatipu High School U14 rugby season 2016. Training is every Tuesday and Thursday at 4pm, don't be late."

"Yesss," shouted Anaru to himself as he punched the air.

The mist that had cloaked the entire area, hiding the mountain peaks of the Southern Alps from view earlier, had evaporated as the summer sun had melted the mist away, giving rise to what promised to be another beautiful summer's day. A few bees were frantically buzzing around a small clump of late flowering Lupins down by the water's edge, collecting the last of the nectar. Their bright vivid colours of deep purple, pale pinks, blues, creams and yellows blended in nicely against the strong turquoise blue of the sky and the dark blue waters of the lake as they gently swayed in the light breeze blowing on the shore.

The tranquillity of Lake Wakatipu was shattered as the powerful outboard motors of the thunder jet ripped their way across the water's surface, sending wash hither and thither as the speed jet zigzagged its way to the wooden jetty at Walter Peak, where Anaru was standing. His eldest sister, who with her partner owned and ran the thunder jet business. Anaru appreciated the time his sister had taken out of her busy schedule to pick him up; he'd initially planned on taking the ninety minute ferry crossing on the TSS Earnslaw like he normally did, spending the time reading the latest book he had ordered off the internet about the most recent laws the rugby authorities had introduced this season. But clearly his sister had other ideas. Pulling alongside the jetty, his sister shouted at him to jump in and throw the red life jacket on.

Gently pulling back on the throttle and turning the wheel, Anaru, with his sister positioned directly behind him, steered the powerboat away from the jetty and headed out to the deeper waters of the lake, where he was able to bring the boat to almost full power. The boat ate up the water as it skimmed and bounced at great speed across the lake surface. His sister could see the smile on his face but she quickly grabbed his hand to ease back on the throttle as a thunder jet, like a big beast, could easily flip over in inexperienced hands. Anaru was enjoying the ride of his life; all he could think about was the faces of his friends as he came into the small harbour at Queenstown. Quad biking he was used too, as he would often go with his father and the farm hands on his better days rounding up the sheep on the steep hillsides. Rightly or wrongly he assumed that steering the speed boat would be similar to riding the quad bike; like any twelve-year old lad, the dangers of flipping never entered his head. He just wanted the thrill of the ride.

All his friends had gathered at the café that fronted the shingle beach; cool milkshakes, french fries and different burgers all smothered in disgusting varieties of sauces were the order of the day. His friends had come to share his celebration. With the selfies posted on to Facebook, Instagram and any other social media outlets he and his friends had registered for done, he headed off for his appointment with Mr O'Connell. Anaru checked the time on his phone; he realised he was going to be late and, remembering the text he had received that morning about punctuality, he raced through the town streets, shouting at people to get out of his way. Fryer St was directly ahead; with moments to spare, having sprinted the entire length of the street, he reached the school gates in the nick of time.

"Hmm… maybe I should put you on the wing, Anaru, following that impressive spurt!"

Anaru hadn't got the energy to reply, huffing and puffing to catch his breath; he was out of condition. All the chemo, radiotherapy and drugs over the last few years had taken it out of him, leaving him physically weak. Some serious training would be required; no doubt Mr O'Connell had that firmly in hand. Rummaging around the bottom of his rucksack, Anaru pulled out the plastic bag he had his fifty-five New Zealand dollars in, along with the letter from his parents.

"So, Anaru, you want to be the next Dan Carter? Fly-half for The All Blacks…"

"Yes, sir."

"Well, training starts tomorrow, 4pm sharp, on those fields across there where you played your Rippa Rugby four years ago."

"I know, sir, but that was the non-contact days. I'm going to get my head kicked in now. I need to toughen up."

"Yep… Oh, Anaru."

"Yes."

"Don't turn up to training at the last moment. That's rude. OK?"

With that veiled threat, Anaru shuffled off at a leisurely pace back into town. He looked at his registration form. An elderly man walking his dog was heading in his direction. Anaru stopped him and asked if he would mind taking a photo of him holding his registration form. The elderly man obliged.

"I'll take a few, just to make sure. Now what button do I press on this smartphone of yours?"

Anaru selected the picture that he thought would best reflect his good side; not that he was a poser in any way, but one had to think of image. The other snapshots he deleted; he had enough photos blocking up his phone. Clicking on Dr Smith's team's email address, he sent the image of himself holding his registration documents. He tagged a message to the picture:

'To Dr Smith. Today is a new day in my new life, the life you and your team gave back to me; the last three years have been so challenging. I wanted to personally thank you for what you all did for me; you have no idea what it means to me to be able to play my rugby. I want to thank you from the bottom of my heart and thought the best way to do this was by sending you a photo of myself and to let you know my training to become New Zealand's fly-half in years to come starts tomorrow. Oh, by the way, you can see that my hair has started to come back. I'll need a haircut soon. Can't wait to go to the barbers and get my haircut. Thank you love Anaru.'

It was a glorious summer's day as he ambled his way back to the café on the lakeside where all his friends were still sitting. His sister had promised him and his friend Pete a parasailing lesson and that was an offer he was taking up. As he neared the café he could see that his friend Pete was already togged up and that his wetsuit was folded across the yellow plastic chair next to the bins. The two of them were so excited; they had seen many visitors come to Queenstown and enjoy the thrill of the ride. Today was their turn. Fully kitted and harnessed in, the speed jet slipped its mooring and headed for the open water of the lake. With full throttle on and the bright orange and blue canopy with a smiley face on fully open, Anaru and his friend Pete were lifted off the jet, high in to the air. It was exhilarating as the wind tore at their faces, the speedboat below them zigzagging and swivelling in all directions, adding to the fun. But like most things in life the ride came to an end; Anaru and his friend Pete disrobed and returned to the party.

Anaru looked at the messages on his phone; his father had texted to say that he had booked a table at the Sky Gondola restaurant for all the family and for him to be at the cable car terminal at 7pm for the ride up to the restaurant. His mother would bring a change of clothes.

That's cool, he loved going up there for dinner. The view across the mountains and the lake were spectacular.

Two messages appeared; they were from the former All Black Players Dan Carter and Richie McCaw.

'*Well done mate, brill news, I've got two tickets for you and your dad to watch The All Blacks v Wales at the Westpac Stadium, Wellington on 18th July 2016. Don't forget to sing the National Anthem. God defend New Zealand. Oh if you want to sing the Welsh National Anthem, Land of my Fathers, then you had better download it from the Internet. Dan C.*'

'Wow, what fantastic news son!!!. Well done. I've arranged for the latest All Black kit to be sent to your school with your name on the back. Wear it with pride mate!! Richie.'

How did they know, pondered Anaru? I bet my father had something to do with this, he thought.

Mark O'Connell sent a group text out to all the guys, *'Just to let you all know, some of the Otago Highlander players are at the school tomorrow and the talent scouts will be looking for new recruits for the future. So be on time, especially you Anaru.'*

Summer holidays Anaru loved, but this had been a very special and emotional day for him. Three years of battling leukaemia had come to an end and he could now face a new future; a future playing rugby, with the aspiration of one day playing fly-half for New Zealand.

SAIF AND ZAHID

Saif sat alongside his brother Zahid; the once small back street café in Aleppo had been the life and soul of the neighbourhood, but all that remained now was a bombed-out shell, much like all the buildings that once stood proudly on that street. A layer of dust covered the red plastic tablecloth and the purple chairs. Last night's air raids had been particularly bad; the Russian fighter jets tore up the night sky, dropping their bombs indiscriminately. The devastation was clear to see as great plumes of smoke still billowed high above the city. Saif could hear the ambulance sirens still wailing in the background, no doubt taking people to what remained of the various city hospitals.

The Syrian war was now in its fifth year and, like many children of his and Zahid's age, the conflict had left its mark. Their parents had been killed years ago, leaving the two brothers to survive on the streets of Aleppo amidst the bombs and the bullets. Saif, being the elder of the two, now twelve, had always felt responsible for his younger brother who, from the age of two, had developed Muscular Dystrophy and was now wheelchair bound. The street shelter they had lived in for the last few months with other abandoned street kids had taken a direct hit the other night. The shelter that was home for himself and Zahid was ruined beyond recognition. Many of his friends had died that night. He and Zahid only survived by sleeping in their usual place, under the old concrete block supported by stones that acted as legs, creating a kind of table. The table took the brunt of the falling masonry. Dazed and badly wounded, the emergency services managed to pull him and Zahid out alive.

Saif remembered sitting in the back of the ambulance, covered in blood and debris, looking at the large gash in his brother's right leg; he equally called to mind the screaming of other children everywhere in the hospital corridors waiting for attention. He recalled running around desperately, trying to get the nurse's attention, begging, screaming at them to look at Zahid's leg. He knew without immediate help Zahid would have bled to death in hours. Two things street life had taught Saif; look after number one and fight hard to protect what little you had.

The little bombed out café had been home for the last two days, having been patched up by the medical staff at the hospital and turfed out back onto the streets. For Zahid, being eight, life was extremely challenging living in a war torn country and having to cope with his condition, which now confined him to a wheelchair. Life was tough but, like Saif, he too had learnt the art of surviving the streets of Aleppo; he knew living off people's sympathy alone would get him nowhere in life. Drawing on his wits, he spotted the other night in the hospital a battered old wheelchair that an old lady had got out off to go to the toilet. Scraping himself along the floor and dragging himself into the chair he shouted at Saif and, within minutes, the two brothers had scarpered out of the hospital, vanishing down the back streets into thin air.

Zahid looked up to see what was making the loud rumbling noise that was also shaking the buildings along the street; to his astonishment it was a Syrian armoured tank. The tank he was used to seeing prowling round the streets of his city Aleppo, but what surprised him was the fact it was being driven and controlled by a group of teenage youths. It rumbled past the two brothers and the three heavily-armed, spotty-faced boys that sat on top of the tank waved as if acknowledging Saif and Zahid. Within minutes the armoured tank came to an abrupt stop. The youths jumped down from the tank and two more crawled out from the tank's inner belly. Zahid shouted at Saif to push him down the street to where the tank had stopped; to both brothers' shock they watched the lads strip off and jump into what appeared to be a small crater filled with fresh water. Saif acknowledged the look on Zahid's face; both of them knew the streets around here like the back of their hands and couldn't recall seeing this pool before. Instantaneously Saif jumped into the water crater, having carefully removed his bandages. Zahid simply sat and watched all the frolickings of enjoyment. It was good to see Saif having a few moments of fun, plus like himself Saif was beginning to stink and a good wash wouldn't go amiss; he only wished he could join them. Zahid was amazed to see the guys had brought along their own shower gel. A couple of the lads had clambered out of the small crater and started to remove the scraps of clothes he was wearing, gently picking him up and lowering him to the others, taking care to ensure his heavily bandaged right leg was held high to ensure it was kept dry. The so-called bath was a welcome relief, but as the others drove off in the armoured tank Saif had worked out that the hole must have been created by one of last night's bombs that hit the city and that the explosion had ruptured a main water pipe, filling the hole nicely and creating the small public swimming bath.

The day was hotting up; both Saif and Zahid knew their wet bodies would soon dry out with the day's heat, so quickly threw on the rags they had for clothes. Saif noticed a piece of paper tucked under the cushion of Zahid's newly acquired chair; pulling it from under his brother, Saif quickly read the message.

'Payment received! Al-Otrosh Mosque front steps Friday.'

Saif knew exactly what this message meant and so did Zahid. The old lady whose chair they had cunningly stolen the other night had been in touch with underground organisations to get herself, and no doubt some of her family, out of Syria, the most likely destination being somewhere in Europe. The world had come to know these organisations as unscrupulous people traffickers. Do they care who they rip off? No. Would they check the identification of those they were moving around! Probably not. The thought crossed both brothers' minds: could this be an unexpected escape plan? A route to a better, safer, life? Where would they go? The UK, Sweden, Germany possibly? With these thoughts racing through their minds they headed to the mosque. Today was Friday, the day of prayer for those that followed the Muslim faith.

Saif had broken into a sweat as he pushed his brother through the war torn streets of Aleppo. For Zahid the ride was bumpy and rough, but he had become accustomed to this mode of transport; he knew that the long road to Europe would be extremely challenging. He had seen the pictures from the TV; the images that were beamed around the world showing children like him dying from starvation and exhaustion or drowning in the Mediterranean Sea. For him and Saif this was a risk worth taking, as there was nothing for them here in Aleppo. Tomorrow a barrel bomb or a sniper's bullet could kill both of them.

The blue ribbon that had been tied to the left handle of the wheelchair had perplexed Saif. Now he was beginning to think it was some kind of code. Would the people traffickers be looking for a wheelchair with a blue ribbon? Curiosity had got the better of him.

Friday being the day of prayer meant the area around the Mosque was predictably busy. The brothers waited patiently by the steps, as the message hadn't given a specific time. It was late evening when a man and a woman, heavily disguised by red keffiyehs across their faces, pulled up in an battered old green van. The woman wound down the window and shouted a couple of names. Saif assumed that these names were something to do with the old lady. With nothing to lose, Saif pushed Zahid towards the van, but as he did so he felt a sharp cosh on the head; as he fell to the ground he could faintly hear a groan from Zahid. Rightly or wrongly he assumed Zahid had been knocked unconscious like himself. Clearly the traffickers were taking no chances with being identified and had taken the necessary precautions.

As Saif came round, he started to realise that he was blindfolded and that his arms and feet had been tied together with what he could only assume was some kind of tape. An instant panic flashed across his mind; where was Zahid? He moved slightly to his right and, as he did so, he could feel the spokes of a wheel brushing against his right arm; shuffling forward he could feel the warmth of a leg and, with a huge sigh of relief, he quietly whispered his brother's name. Moments later a muffled voice responded. 'Saif, you there bro?' The rocking motion of the van started to make Saif sick, but he restrained himself from throwing up as he didn't want to draw attention to himself. The two brothers kept whispering messages of comfort to each other. How long they had been travelling for and where were they neither of them had any idea.

What felt like an eternity came to an abrupt end. The van screeched to a halt. Zahid could hear the van's front doors being opened and slammed shut; he could also hear raised voices outside. All of a sudden the back doors opened and a sharp blast of cold air swept its way in, giving a welcome breath of freshness. The night air swiftly brought both brothers to their full senses. Saif could feel a sharp knife tugging at the tape that had bound his arms and legs; a note was thrust into his trouser pocket but what was on it would have to wait for a few minutes. Still blindfolded, Saif could hear the van disappear into the middle of the night. Who brought himself and Zahid to this precise spot he would never know, nor did he care.

Saif and Zahid had no idea how long they were unconscious for; had they been drugged? All they knew was they were confused, exhausted and starving. The only possessions they owned in the world were the tattered rags of clothes they had on. Saif quietly turned to a small group of women and children. He asked a young mother who was breastfeeding a small baby, where were they?

"You're on a beach, sweetheart."

"Which beach?"

"A small beach just up from Dikili on the Turkish coastline."

Saif stared at Zahid; he could see the terror in his brother's eyes. Both of them had seen the TV images of small inflatable boats battling against the elements of the cruel Aegean sea, boats capsizing, the lucky ones picked up by the rescue boats and the rest taken by the sea never to be seen or heard again. Zahid took Saif's right hand.

"We have no choice, Saif; nothing to go back to."

"I know."

The crossing to the Greek Island of Lesbos was going to be perilous, even if the waters were calm. Still holding his brother's hand, Zahid looked into his brother's eyes.

"If the boat sinks, let me go and save yourself."

No more words were needed; they both knew, living with Muscular Dystrophy, Zahid would struggle to swim.

All of a sudden a great commotion welled up amongst the crowd as the noise of two outboard motors could be heard tearing up the waters of the small bay. Two bright orange inflatable boats came into sight. The crowd surged forward, surrounding the boats, women screaming at their children to stay close. A rather rude big man yelled at the top of his voice.

"We're not taking that wheelchair. Get him out of it."

It was every man for himself as the crowds waded out to the boats, children clambering aboard, shouting at their friends to hurry up. Saif, from nowhere, found the strength to lift Zahid out of his wheelchair and place him over his right shoulder. Struggling, he managed to wade into the water and, on reaching the first boat, two women hauled Zahid on to the boat. Saif heaved himself on board; Zahid had wriggled his way into the centre, thinking that this would be the safest place. Life jackets were handed around, but there weren't enough for everybody. Zahid turned to Saif.

"You wear it."

The body of the inflatable moulded itself to

the gentle up and down swells of the sea, but that didn't last for long. Dawn had broken, revealing a dullish grey day; as the morning progressed the gentle swells intensified as the waters around them became choppy. Saif could see the other inflatable boat ahead of them, bobbing up and down with the strengthening waves. The wind had picked up and people started to become agitated; the panic on a few faces started to show as the boat began taking on water. The water was sloshing around people's feet; several youngsters had started to bale out the water with various plastic containers that were to hand. Saif seized a large plastic tub that a young family had brought with them; grabbing it he frantically started to bale out some of the water swishing around his feet. The situation was getting desperate; more water was being taken on board than could be baled out; the outcome would be inevitable, but how long had they got before the vessel sank? A powerful speedboat appeared from nowhere, pulling alongside both inflatables; the people traffickers clearly didn't want to be caught by the Greek Authorities so abandoned ship, leaving the innocent people in the boats to the mercy of the sea. As fast as the powerboat arrived it disappeared.

The inflatable only lasted another hour. The attempt to keep the boat afloat, at least until the Greek coastline was in sight, failed. Squeals of panic could be heard everywhere as mothers tried desperately to cling to their children. The waters were bitterly cold; those that had life jackets clung to others to give what little support they could. Saif had managed to set the two flares off; a young girl had noticed them when she got on the boat and had passed them to Saif for safekeeping. Zahid prayed that the red vapour trail given off by the flares that soared into the sky would attract the attention of any ships within the immediate vicinity. The coldness of the water was the biggest killer and both brothers knew that. Saif hung on to Zahid, but as time slipped by he found it increasingly difficult to keep hold of the brother who meant so much to him. At times Zahid would slip under the water as the swell of the sea engulfed them; Saif would redouble his effort and manage to retrieve Zahid, but for how long he could do this? He knew in his heart the answer was not for much longer. Zahid had said when the moment came to let him go and save himself.

Saif, exhausted, wet, hungry and in the depths of despair, must have passed out temporarily for he did not see or hear the Greek rescue boat that had come alongside him. Looking frantically around him he couldn't see Zahid. A large hand grabbed him by the scruff of his neck and plucked him out of the sea. A silver foil sheet was draped around him; looking at the man straight in the face he whispered, 'My brother.' The Greek man placed his large hands around Saif's face, gently turning Saif's head to see a small body wrapped in tin foil being gently warmed by two women. It was Zahid. They had survived, and they were alive.

The port of Mytilini, the main town on the

Greek Island of Lesbos, was thriving with the daily hustle and bustle of life. Sitting huddled together in their tin foil blankets aboard the rescue boat, Saif and Zahid watched with trepidation as the boat pulled alongside the harbour walls. Cruise ships and the island ferry boats filled the small port, as well as little fishing boats belonging to the locals bobbing up and down in the water. On the quayside was a well-drilled team of volunteers used to the sight of the rescue boats bringing desperate refugee children from war torn Syria. The two brothers sat quietly on a little bench. Saif had already had a quiet word with one of the volunteer workers, who wore a bright yellow T-shirt with the letters UNHCR printed on the front in blue. Moments later the young girl came back with a small wheelchair. Zahid, still traumatised, asked the young lady, "Do you work for the United Nations?"

"No, I'm a volunteer."

"Where do you come from?"

"France."

"Whereabouts?"

''Paris.''

"Oh! Perhaps Saif and myself will go there."

"Wow, but let's get you and your brother sorted out first, OK?"

"Cool."

Saif spotted the big Greek gentleman that had plucked him out of the sea; gently getting up he walked along the quayside. With a slight tap on the shoulder the big man turned around and Saif held out his hand.

"I want to thank you for pulling me out of the sea." The tears flowed down his cheeks as he asked, "What happened to the other women and children in the boat?"

The tall Greek man knelt down, took Saif's small frail hands into his own huge hands and looked Saif in the eye.

"I'm so sorry, young man, but we were too late; a lot of the children drowned along with their mothers."

Saif slumped to the ground and completely broke down in tears. The big Greek man scooped him up in his arms and held him tight. This moment of tenderness from someone Saif had never met before was the most comforting feeling he had known in a long time.

A small room at the back of the rescue centre was Saif and Zahid's next port of call; thousands of migrants and refugees had started the process here to enter the EU for a better life. Saif wheeled his brother in; both of them told the story of what had happened to them and where they wanted to go. The look of astonishment from the team of people that sat on the other side of the table, hearing what plans the brothers had, was a picture to behold. It was agreed that the normal camp designated for orphaned child refugees would be too dangerous for Zahid with his physical disabilities. Reports had started to emerge over the last few days of infighting and assaults on Syrian child refugees from Afghan and Iraqi children; refugees themselves having being forced to leave their own countries due to violence and persecution. Drug gangs had infiltrated the camp, spreading their evil ways; bullying and blackmail was rife. The police had been called into deal with the matter. The perimeter fence, on numerous occasions, had been knocked down and those children that escaped were still at large, probably in another country by now.

The Polka camp, with its wooden buildings and tents shaded from the sun by the surrounding pine trees, would be a better choice; there the two boys could rest from their ordeal for a while, have their needs assessed and supported. By registering with the Greek Authorities they could get the ferry to Athens and from there to the destination of their dreams. For Saif and Zahid that would be Sweden.

All the best lads.

GUIA

It was 4am; the reminder call on her mobile phone had gone off. With bleary eyes she quietly rolled herself out of bed, tossing the duvet aside. Two messages and one Facebook notification showed on the phone; her Twitter account had been extraordinarily quiet throughout the night, much to her dismay. Kaahi was already up and sitting at the family table, fitting his prosthetic leg to his stump. He had come to Brazil from Somalia three years ago as an illegal immigrant. The war that had been raging there for several years had not only destroyed his homeland, but also left him orphaned; homeless and without his left leg beneath his kneecap. The mine he had stood on had totally destroyed all the bone and tissues. The decision to amputate was taken by one of the top surgeons at the main hospital in Mogadishu, Somalia's capital city.

Guia had first noticed Kaahi sitting amongst the down-and-outs in one of the narrow alleyways where she and her father delivered soup to the homeless in the nearby favela. What struck her most about Kaahi was how polite, clean and well-spoken he was; the normal response from the street people was aggression and foul language, often caused by the side-effects of alcohol and drugs. For weeks she and her father would do the evening soup run, and every night Kaahi would wait in the same place for his soup and whatever Guia and her father had managed to scrounge from the local shops and cafes. He was in pain from the infection that had infiltrated his stump; Guia could see the pain etched on his face. One night, walking home, she told her father about the young Somali boy and his desperate plight; she explained to her father how she had taken the time to get to know Kaahi, that his dream was to take part in the 2016 Paralympics there in Rio De Janeiro, a city known to the world as simply Rio.

The following morning Guia's father had made a decision; they would trawl the favela back streets looking for Kaahi. Her father knew that if gangrene had taken hold Kaahi wouldn't survive much longer. It was late afternoon when Guia spotted a bundle of rags, propped up against the sides of a dilapidated wooden hut whose orange faded sides had been heavily daubed with honour badges from one of the local gangs. It was the green stick wedged between the window and the doorframe that Guia instantly recognised; carefully pulling back the tattered rags two frightened dark eyes stared back at her; it was Kaahi, the young, twelve-year-old emaciated black boy. Guia tapped him gently on the shoulder; looking slightly dazed and shielding his eyes from the bright afternoon sun he smiled at Guia, exposing a wonderful set of white African teeth.

"Kaahi, you are coming to live with us. End of."
"Why, Guia?"
"You just are."

The small shanty house she shared with her father and three sisters consisted of a small kitchen to the front, along with a moderately sized living room that led onto a small terrace that was littered with small model houses made out of breeze block or milk crates painted in bright pinks, yellows, greens and purples. It was a hobby her mother had until she passed away two years ago. The three small bedrooms that sat directly above the living room were accessed by a hole in the ceiling through which a ladder was placed. For the toilet and washing facilities; well, that was a trip to their aunt's four doors down.

It was clear for all to see that Kaahi's leg was badly infected and that he needed urgent medical treatment. The look on her father's face said it all; getting treatment at the local hospitals would be difficult, as Kaahi had no identification papers or money.

It was early evening and the storms that had been promised had arrived. Guia went to her room; the noise the rain made as it pelted down on the corrugated roof was deafening. Her bed was the bottom bunk and under it was a gold box; in it was a blue bank passbook. Pulling it out and scrambling down the ladder she showed her father how much was in her account. Her father was astonished; he had an inkling that she had an account but how much was in the account shocked him.

"How… have you managed to accumulate all this money?"

"Father! I have been writing short stories and putting them on Amazon. What I make from the stories goes to my business bank account each month, so you see I have enough money to pay for a private doctor at one of the smart clinics near the beach at Copacabana."

"But you don't have a computer, so how…?"

"I go to an internet café after school each day down by the beach. The money I have made was to go towards a laptop and a mobile phone, so I could write my stories from home."

"We'll talk about this later, but for now you need to go and get an appointment for Kaahi."

With the threat of further discussions with her father re the money in her bank account, she left for the smart part of Copacabana. She knew how the conversation with her father would go, but she would stand her ground, for this money was hers, her future and escape from the poverty-stricken violent favela she lived in.

The appointment with the consultant next morning was brief; Kaahi was given a course of antibiotics to clear up the infection, with a further appointment made for two weeks time to see what further treatments would be required, if necessary of course.

Guia knew about Kaahi's dream to become a gold medal winner in the Rio 2016 Paralympics; she also knew that to run for Brazil, Kaahi would have to become a Brazilian citizen. How to register for citizenship and what procedures to follow she had no idea, but the government website on Brazilian Citizenship would be a good place to start.

"Where're we going, Guia?"

"To the internet café."

"Why?"

"Firstly to look up and print off the guidelines of how to make you a Brazilian, and secondly to see who are the best trainers/coaches to help you get your gold medal."

"Why are you doing this for me? Nobody has cared about me, here or back in Somalia."

"I may only be nine years old, but I have ambitions. My sisters might want to stay in the slums and drag up their children here, but I don't. I want to make something of my life, challenge the world, be someone. I saw something in you that I haven't seen on the streets around here; someone with a dream, a goal in life. I want to help you achieve that gold medal dream, challenge, whatever."

"Wow, you're one gutsy lady."

"Yep, I'm going places. You never know – by drawing attention to your running abilities, someone might take notice of me one day and coach me to be an Olympic gold medallist in the Tokyo Games 2020."

"Cool."

"Plus, I looked up on the Internet, the world's greatest runners come from Somalia, Ethiopia, Kenya and that part of East Africa."

"What if the Brazilian authorities reject my application?"

"Then we will challenge them; if necessary you'll have to run as an independent athlete and compete under the Olympic Flag."

"How do you know that?"

"I've done my research."

The Internet café was busy. Sitting in her favourite spot Guia logged on to her account; she hated that little circle that appeared in the middle of the screen, as if buffering round and round. Frustrated while waiting for the wi-fi connection to kick in, she turned to Kaahi.

"How did you get to Brazil from Somalia?"

"Long story."

"Well?"

"A friend's father worked at the airport on the freight side; for the right money I was smuggled onto the cargo deck in a crate. The flight was to Rio. I was discovered by the custom officials at the airport and handed over to the local authorities. They placed me in a children's home; it was an awful place, so I ran away."

The three years Kaahi had lived in the household had seen many achievements, along with numerous drawbacks from the various government departments. Getting Kaahi into schools and finding the right coaches with suitable training programmes adapted to Kaahi's needs had been tough going at times. With each challenge faced and overcome, Guia found herself sitting across the breakfast table at 4am on this wet, miserable, damp and dark morning. The trophies that were scattered around the room highlighted Kaahi's success in the two hundred and four hundred metre sprint track events he had run in over the last few years, both in Brazil and overseas. With his citizenship granted and all his accomplishments in sprinting, he had drawn the attention of the various Brazilian sporting organisations and was shortlisted to represent Brazil in the Rio games in the T44 two hundred and four hundred metre track events. Guia's money from the sale of her books on Amazon had gone some way to supporting the gold medal dream. Small sponsorships along with donations from friends kept Kaahi's hopes and aspirations of being an Paralympic champion alive.

The games were three months away, but the punishing training programme still had to be maintained on a daily basis. The city of Rio was abuzz with excitement as the opening ceremony loomed ever nearer. Guia opened the door; she was not looking forward to her run alongside Kaahi and the others. Taking a brief moment she looked down out across the city that lay sprawled beneath her and across the harbour; the two most famous landmarks known to the entire world that gave Rio its identity dominated the skyline. On her left was the illuminated statue of Christ the Redeemer, standing thirty metres in height and perched seven hundred metres up on the Corcovado Mountain. To her right was Sugarloaf Mountain, a block of granite rising from the sea to a height of approximately four hundred metres. In a few hours time, when the rain clouds had evaporated and the sun had positioned itself high in the sky, thousands of tourists would flock to these iconic symbols, have their photos taken and immediately download them on to Facebook and other various social media sites for all their friends to see. Would these tourists come and visit her shack of a home high on the hillside of one of the poorest favelas that surrounded the city? She doubted it very much. The tour operators and the police would have advised them to stay well away for fear of being shot.

Kaahi had sprinted off down the narrow streets; his new prosthetic leg with the carbon fibre blade had been specially adapted for him. His last prosthetic leg had taken several weeks to get used to. This one he needed to get used to sharpish; any adjustments that were needed would have to be sorted out quickly as the Paralympics were just around the corner. Two legs had been ordered; the second was for emergencies in case of unforeseen circumstances, mainly to cover theft. The legs were expensive, costing over eight thousand US Dollars for two; the gangs that prowled the streets could easily get a fair price on the black market and with the money buy more drugs to feed the habit of the rich that lived in the skyscrapers down near the harbour.

Guia looked on with pride as she watched Kaahi and his running mates disappear from her view; she was no match for her so-called adopted brother. The emaciated figure she and her father brought home three years ago had turned into the highly toned body of a future Paralympic champion. The lads that ran with Kaahi were from the same running club, but didn't have the same desires or ambitions in life. They knew what the training plan was for the morning; normally Guia ran with Kaahi, but today was one of her off days. She had told him at breakfast if she wasn't able to keep up with him he was to wait at the lower end of Copacabana beach. Kaahi's running mates also acted as bodyguards, fending off any unwanted paparazzi that lurked around the many hidden alleyways and street corners. As the games neared, the media intrusion on potential athletes increased; some attention was welcome, some was not.

Many of Guia's friends saw her as a determined young lady; despite her young age of twelve she had an astute business brain. She texted a few of her friends, explaining she was running on her own as Kaahi had gone ahead. She knew which mates would have their mobiles switched on and that the phone would be on the pillow or within arm's reach. Within minutes two boys who sat behind her in school were by her side, dishevelled and grumpy, there to protect her from any undesirable characters roaming the streets at this early hour of the day. Her phone pinged and she stopped to read a text from Kaahi.

'TV crews out at beach.'

Copacabana beach was quiet at this time of the morning, for the party revellers from last night had gone home by now and the tourists and locals that would later flock in their hundreds to soak up the sun and ride the waves were still in their beds. Guia spotted the TV vans parked up; she knew Kaahi and the others ahead would have brushed them off. What was important to Kaahi was getting the attention of the Paralympic committee and winning his races over the next few meets, not chatting to TV presenters looking for stories to put on their live breakfast shows that morning. Guia understood the power of the media; she knew the more media coverage an athlete got, the better the sponsorship deals from the big corporate companies would be, but that athlete would need to ensure the gold medals would go round their necks and not their rivals'. Guia crossed over the road and knocked on the doors of several of the TV vans. A few of the TV crews politely told her to go away, but those that expressed an interest she happily gave interviews, telling them how Kaahi arrived in Brazil and how he had got to where he was now.

Over the next few weeks the daily routine continued. Kaahi stuck to the rigorous training plan put in place by his coaching team and won all his races, putting him in a strong position with the Paralympic committee. Guia went on various TV shows talking about Kaahi; she also took advantage of the social media avenues that were freely available, posting several videos of Kaahi training on YouTube. She even went as far as writing a short story about him and downloaded that on to Amazon for all her readers that had bought her stories over the years to read about.

It was mid-July, the day that the Paralympic select committees would make their decisions as to who would be in the squad to represent Brazil at the Rio Paralympic games 2016. It was a long day; friends kept texting both Guia and Kaahi asking whether they had heard anything from the committee. The tension around the living room was mounting as the day went on. The table that Guia and Kaahi had chatted over and eaten around for the last three years was getting crowded as friends and family gathered throughout the day. Finally the call they had been waiting for came through at 3pm. Kaahi recognised the number on the screen; taking a deep breath he pressed the accept button, stood up and walked outside onto the terrace that had all Guia's late mother's brightly coloured model houses on. The room went silent. Guia hovered by the back door, anxious to see the look on Kaahi's face as he carefully listened to the voice on the other end. A smile steadily crept across Kaahi's face, showing those beautiful white African teeth of his. Putting the phone down on a plant pot he turned to Guia:

"T44 two hundred and four hundred metres Rio 2016 HERE I COME!!!."

Guia took a step back and leant against the wall. He had done it, she had done it, they had done it; a poor black boy from East Africa was going to represent Brazil on the world stage at the Rio 2016 Paralympic Games. At the age of fifteen Kaahi was off to the greatest games of his life. Tomorrow he and Guia would head off to Sao Paulo, where the Brazilian Paralympic Committee was going to announce to the public who had been selected and for what event.

Two months had almost passed from the day

Kaahi had been officially told he had been selected. Training had been rigorous but today, the 7th September 2016, he would walk into the Maracana stadium behind the Brazilian flag. Being the host nation, the Brazilian team would be the last team to enter the world famous stadium in the Parade of Nations. This year approximately one hundred and sixty countries were being represented, roughly four thousand four hundred athletes. This was going to be a wonderful spectacle.

Kaahi's moment had come, dressed like most of the other Brazilian athletes in his green suit with splashes of yellow and blue on his jacket. The long wait was worth it as he entered the tunnel. He could hear the roar of the dignitaries, overseas spectators and of course the Brazilian supporters who had packed the seventy-eight thousand-seater stadium to the rafters. The noise was electrifying as the crowd spotted the green, yellow and blue of the Brazilian flag entering the stadium.

Guia and her father had taken up their seats; this was a moment Guia had dreamed of for years. She could see Kaahi taking pictures on his phone. Pride swelled up inside her and a little tear rolled down her cheek. Her father gently turned to her and, with a large finger, delicately wiped the tear away. With all the athletes in place the ceremony continued, a large image of a pulsating heart attracting everybody's attention. it was supposed to represent the life, passion and spirit of each Paralympic athlete. Tomorrow the games would start.

The Olympic Stadium was in the Maracana zone, a short distance from the Olympic Village where most of the Brazilian team had based themselves. Kaahi's coach and mentor had always told him that on the big occasions race tactics and mental attitude were as important as timing. Guia and the team that had been put in place to support him knew that Kaafi's youthful inexperience was a weak point and that the other athletes racing against him today would exploit that, as they were more experienced runners. It was a well-known fact that an athlete could be the best in his field, but on the day what counted most was the athlete's mental attitude and belief in him or herself. Tactics and frame of mind was a discussion Guia and Kaahi often had around the breakfast table at 4am in the morning as they prepared for the first of the daily runs. Kaahi was aware of what the people around him were saying and he felt confident that his head was in the right place for next few days.

Storm clouds had gathered over the Olympic Stadium; Guia looked up from her place at trackside and, seeing the deep black threatening clouds hovering above, quietly prayed to herself that the clouds would hang on to their watery contents for a few more minutes. The first of the T44 200 metre qualifying races was about to start. The names of the competitors and the countries they represented were read out over the stadium speakers. Kaahi was in lane three, a good lane to have. As his name was read out a large cheer went up in the stadium, Kaahi waved at the crowd, acknowledging their support before settling down and waiting for the starter's pistol to go off. They were off; the roar of the crowd filled Kaahi's head as he sprinted round the bend. He could feel and see the other athletes around him but as long as he stayed within spitting distance of his main rival from the USA, he stood a good chance of getting to the final. Guia jumped up and down in her seat, shouting her head off as Kaahi entered the back straight, but something wasn't right. Kaahi stumbled. He appeared to lose control of his blade and became unbalanced; face down on the track and not finishing meant Kaahi's medal hopes for the two hundred metres were gone. Guia saw the look of frustration and disappointment written all over his face and wondered how they would begin to put the sparkle back into his confidence to face the T44 400 challenge tomorrow. A despondent Kaahi sat down at the side of the track; the support team, still in shock at what had happened, came alongside him. All Guia could do was watch from her seat. Kaahi explained what he thought had gone wrong; the fitting of his prosthetic leg around his stump for some reason didn't feel right and had become loose going round the bend. Closer examination by the team proved that the issue was not the prosthetic leg but Kaahi's inexperience on the day. In all of his excitement he had simply not ensured his stump was properly secured in the socket. Lesson learnt.

Kaahi was angry with himself for making such a stupid mistake, a mistake he was never going to repeat. Today he had another opportunity to prove himself; with his prosthetic leg properly fitted and checked by Guia and his coach, he walked out onto the track with more determination than ever to qualify for the 400 metre final on Friday afternoon. This time running in lane two, he lined up on the starting blocks. The strategy was firmly in his head, where to be at the various stages of the race and which rivals to keep an eye on. The pistol had gone off, the roar of the crowd he'd completely blocked out; he was on track, the plan was working and his main rivals where were they should be. All he needed to do was maintain his position, stay upright and focus on the finish line. He was delighted he had come first, which went against the advice from the team and Guia, but for him it was the right decision. With the race over he gathered up his things and left the stadium knowing in his heart he had qualified and headed for the training grounds. For the next few days of his life he would live, sleep and breathe the T44 400 metre final.

Guia was angry; she had texted Kaahi several times over the last two days but he had returned none of her messages. Clearly he had taken the decision to shut himself off from the world and focus on the race of his life. The moment had come; it was Friday afternoon and the final of the T44 400 metres was ten minutes away. Guia and her father had taken their usual seats. She was nervous, tense and still angry with Kaahi, but that anger she would have to put aside as she watched

Kaahi emerge onto the track. In her right hand was the Brazilian flag, which she would hand to Kaahi for his lap of honour; this was a prearranged agreement they had discussed several weeks ago.

The stadium was full. Kaahi was in lane four, a really good lane; his main rival from the USA was in lane three. The other athletes taking part were from Canada, China, New Zealand, Ukraine, South Africa and oddly enough a young guy from Somalia. The crowd cheered as the stadium announcer read out the names of the athletes and where they originated from; a huge cheer erupted as Kaahi's name was mentioned, and he reacted to the crowd by waving his right hand, at the same time smiling revealing his beautiful African teeth. A hush descended across the stadium as the starter raised his hand with the pistol in. The athletes steadied themselves, waiting anxiously for the click of the gun. The pistol was fired and they were off. The New Zealand and South African contenders were off to a good start; so were the Canadian and the Somalia guy. Kaahi and his American rival were in fifth and sixth place. The strategy was going to plan; everybody knew the last sixty metres were the most important. Kaahi could hear the roar of the crowd urging him on and two hundred metres in he and the American had moved up to third and fourth places respectively; at this stage of the race he was in the right position. The early leaders had started to wane a bit. Thirty-three seconds in and approaching the third bend Kaahi and his American rival had manoeuvred themselves into second and third positions, The Chinese guy had started to apply some pressure and was sitting comfortably on their shoulders; as the homestretch approached the Brazilians in the crowd could sense a medal coming on and Kaahi could feel the excitement and tension of the stadium as the crowd screamed at him to keep going. Guia was exhausted with the excitement, jumping up and down, flapping her arms all over the place, goading Kaahi across the winning line. Kaahi could feel the presence of the American and Chinese athletes bearing down on him. His heart was pounding out of his chest, ready to burst, his lungs were on fire and every muscle fibre in his body was stretched to its full potential. He could see the finishing line, his rivals were by his side; somehow he had to find that extra bit of energy from somewhere. Ten metres out and his American contender had taken the edge and was in first place; he prayed for extra energy and from nowhere a surge of power swelled in his aching limbs. He had crossed the line. He knew he had got a medal; what colour it was he didn't know.

Exhausted and mentally spent, he collapsed on the track. Guia had jumped over the security barrier, much to the annoyance of the track officials, not that she cared. She ran to Kaahi, who was still on the ground. The crowd were ecstatic but it was too close to call. Kaahi's coach and team remained calm, daring not to dream what the outcome was going to be. They stared at the scoreboard for what seemed like an eternity; with bated breath they waited and waited. The tension was almost unbearable and then the results came through. The stadium exploded with delight; Brazil had its first gold medal of the games, Kaahi had done it. He had won the gold medal. Brazil took the gold; it was silver for the USA and bronze for China. Kaahi picked himself of the floor, dusted himself down and grabbed the flag from Guia. Draping the flag around himself he headed off on his lap of honour. As he sauntered around the stadium waving at the crowd all he could see was a sea of green, yellow and blue as thousands of flags were being waved about all over the place.

Guia took a few moments to reflect on what had happened. Three years ago this gold medal Paralympic champion was an emaciated African boy that she and her father had scraped off an alleyway in one of the poorest favelas of Rio. All the short stories she had toiled over and sold on Amazon to support Kaahi to achieve his dream, along with the arduous training at all unearthly hours of the day, had paid off. She knew what she wanted from the next four years; a gold medal herself from the Tokyo games 2020.

All that remained was for Kaahi to attend the medal ceremony that night and get his gold medal. The ceremony was brief; Kaahi had got his gold medal. Guia could see the tears of joy flowing down Kaahi's face as he stood on the podium, watching his flag being raised on the stand as the Brazilian national anthem was being played.

Holding his gold medal aloft for the world's

media to photograph him was a proud moment for Kaahi. The press would be anxious to get his story. He caught Guia's eye and, walking across to her, took his medal off and said;

"This is for you, for without you I couldn't have achieved what I have done today. Thank you from the bottom of my heart. Shall we both go to Tokyo 2020 and get you a gold medal as well? Maybe I'll get one for the 200 metres? What do you say?"

"Absolutely."

COMING UP

I hope you enjoyed reading the short stories, and like the characters as much as I enjoyed creating them. The stories are totally fictional with a smattering of facts to give a basic background.

My next book, with yet another five young characters from around the world telling their stories, will follow shortly.

SAY HELLO TO
ANJALA, HAMISH, EMERITA,
DANTEL AND PRIYA.

Anjala is a Nepalese girl from a snow-covered village high in the Himalayan Mountains of the tiny kingdom of Nepal. School is in Pokhara, a small town in the valley below; the daily trek for herself and her brother Rajesh most people would find daunting, having to negotiate steep narrow mountain pathways. It was on a normal day walking down the mountainside she and her brother came across one of the world's most elusive big cats, a snow leopard. Transfixed to the spot as she and her brother get a glimpse of this magnificent cat, she reminds herself what her father has always said if she ever came across this majestic creature, as they are wild, dangerous animals. Anjala is aware what problems these big cats can have if they come into contact with humans, but she is determined to protect her snow leopard and hatches a plan with an Australian TV company that is in the area.

Hamish is my little Scottish character, who along with his friends sets out to protect a royal stag from the trophy hunter's rifles on one of the many Highland estates up in the Cairngorms. Their cunning ways to disrupt the hunt and save the stag is intriguing and leads them in to conflict with the locals, for who culling the herds is a long established tradition.

Emerita is a Swiss girl from Davos in Switzerland. Davos is a small, insignificant town but once a year it comes to the world's attention as political and industrial figures, along with renowned scientists, meet to discuss the world's problems. It's winter and the Alps that surround her town are buried deep in snow. Avalanches are a dangerous and serious threat; to the thousands that converge for this world forum, diplomats, world leaders and TV companies, an avalanche is not high on their agenda. But a sudden avalanche traps the French Ambassador's wife and a small part of her entourage out crosscountry skiing. Emerita's father is the leader for the local mountain rescue team. This is Emerita's first rescue mission, along with her Mount St Bernard dog, as they venture out high in to the Alps to track down the French Ambassadors wife's whereabouts.

Dantel comes from Arequipa, Peru's second city; it sits high in the Andes Mountains in South America. The city is prone to earthquakes, and both he and his orphaned brother Emilio are well versed with what to do if a quake strikes. Despite the warnings, the earthquake strikes and the trail of destruction is huge. Emilio is trapped and Dantel is desperate to find him; using all means available to him he attracts the attention of the rescue teams and manages to ensure Emilio is at the top of their priorities.

Priya is my little blind Indian girl; her family abandoned her at the age of three as the farm the family rented failed to pay its way. Being a blind girl, and from a low caste, she is of little value in Indian society and was left on the side of the road with a simple message attached to her sari to be picked up by a New Zealand backpacker and taken to an orphanage in Amritsar. For years she and her best friend, Neeta, would go to the Sikh Golden Temple and sell the little tapestries they made to the millions of pilgrims and tourists that flocked each year to the Temple. The money she made would go to her evening computer classes. There she would learn the necessary skills to use her specially adapted laptop, which would take her out of abject poverty and fulfil her dream of become a prominent politician on the world stage. The return of her sisters brings back the hurt of her abandonment, but what her sisters see astounds them. They were expecting a pathetic blind girl, but what they see is a determined young woman with aspirations way beyond their imagination.

ACKNOWLEDGEMENTS

Alex Davis for all his tutoring, editing skills and patience.

Mark Bell for his wonderful character illustrations.
www.markbellillustration.com

Camilla Wright for the professional photo. The airbrushing worked.
www.camillawrightphotograpghy.com

Pete Mugleston for his technical skills on the webpage. One of the best friends a guy could have.

MESSAGE

To all my young teenagers that read these five
short stories: thank you.

I hope you enjoy them. If there are any words
you don't understand, ask someone or better still
Google them.

CONTACT

Please feel free to let me know what you think to the stories.

Twitter: John Thomas Crowley @jtcrowley187

Website: www.jtcrowley.com

Facebook: Jtc Crowley

17171061R00040

Printed in Great Britain
by Amazon